Gilbert Francklyn, William Wilberforce

Substance of a Speech Intended to Have Been Made on Mr. Wilberforce's Motion for the Abolition of the Slave Trade

On Tuesday, April 3, 1792

Gilbert Francklyn, William Wilberforce

**Substance of a Speech Intended to Have Been Made on Mr. Wilberforce's Motion
for the Abolition of the Slave Trade**
On Tuesday, April 3, 1792

ISBN/EAN: 9783337405335

Printed in Europe, USA, Canada, Australia, Japan

Cover: Foto ©Andreas Hilbeck / pixelio.de

More available books at **www.hansebooks.com**

SUBSTANCE

OF A

SPEECH

INTENDED TO HAVE BEEN MADE ON

MR. *WILBERFORCE's MOTION*

FOR THE

ABOLITION OF THE SLAVE TRADE,

ON TUESDAY, APRIL 3, 1792:

But the Unwillingness of the Committee to hear any thing farther on the Subject, after Mr. PITT had spoken, prevented the Member from being heard.

SECOND EDITION, CORRECTED,

WITH NOTES, AND AN APPENDIX.

LONDON:

PRINTED FOR J. OWEN, NO. 168, PICCADILLY.

1792.

PREFACE.

SINCE the firſt publication of the following ſheets new Arguments have been
offered to prove the propriety of aboliſhing
the African Trade.

It was aſſerted, in the courſe of the
Debate on the Morning of the 3d Inſtant,
that the King of Denmark had iſſued an
Edict to aboliſh ſuch Trade at the end of
Ten Years. That Edict is now printed
in the Appendix to this edition; by
which it appears, that ſo far from aboliſhing

ing the Commerce, he gives every possible Encouragement to the carrying it on during that term; under an idea that his Colonies being once fully stocked with Negroes, he may not be dependant on other Nations for a supply. Danish Edicts are not like the Laws of the Medes and Persians, irrevocable. The preamble of this Edict, assumes as a principle, that the abolition of the Trade will only be proper WHEN the Danish Colonies are fully supplied.

If that Event should not have happened at the end of the prescribed Term, there can be no doubt but it will be enlarged.

It may not be improper here to observe, that among Mr. Dundas's propositions, one is, to prohibit the carrying Negroes in future

future to Barbadoes, and the ancient Colonies of Antigua, Nevis, St. Kitts, and Montferat, becaufe they do not want them —a meafure certainly nugatory and abfurd. If the inhabitants of thefe Iflands do not want them, no Ships will carry them there. If they do, or fhould want them on account of any particular Calamity, fuch as Hurricanes, Epidemical Diforders, &c. it is unjuft they fhould be deprived of a Commerce allowed to the neighbouring Iflands of St. Vincent, &c. It is to be hoped, before the Meafures now propofed fhall be carried into execution, the Planters and Merchants will have an opportunity of oppofing Facts fairly ftated and afcertained upon Oath, to empty Declamation, and infidious Pretences to Humanity and Juftice.

It

PREFACE.

It is not neceſſary to uſe any arguments to ſhew the impropriety of that Conduct which oppoſes the Cultivation of Lands belonging to Britiſh Subjects, to the great Improvement and Advantage of the Revenues, Commerce and Manufactures of this Country; and to the diminution of the high Price of Sugar, ſo much complained of by the Public.

SUBSTANCE

OF A

SPEECH, &c.

SIR,

A T this late period of the Debate, it is with great reluctance I rife to exprefs my fentiments on a fubject on which fo much has been faid; and faid, too, in fo eloquent a manner, that I fhould not prefume to call the attention of the Committee to any obfervations of mine, if I did not confider it my duty, not only to my Country in general, but to my Conftituents in particular—from a part of whom I alfo have received a petition, praying for the abolition of a Trade, which they qualify with the epithets of *cruel, inhuman,* and *infamous.*

As I know by what fhameful arts this petition was obtained—as I know the greateft part of thofe who have figned it hardly know where Africa is fituated, it is fcarcely pof-

fible

fible thefe people can form any idea of
the circumftances which attend the Traffick carried on in that quarter of the Globe,
but from the falfe accounts artfully fpread
abroad by thofe who call themfelves Aboli-
tionifts. Very few of thofe of my Conftituents, who are men of knowledge and edu-
cation, have figned this Petition : but many
names appear to it I never heard of before,
and therefore fuppofe them to have been obtained in the manner mentioned by my Honourable Friend * on the other fide of the
Houfe. I have, confequently, declined pre-
fenting it.

I fay, Sir, I cannot confider it confiftent
with my duty to give a filent Vote againft the
Propofition of the Honourable Gentleman
who has brought it forward, † as I owe, even
to the leaft informed of my Conftituents, a
reafon why I do not confent to be guided by
their Inftructions, which I fhould think myfelf
bound to do, if the matter was either in any
degree connected with their intereft, or of

---

* Colonel Tarleton,   † Mr. Wilberforce.

which

which they could have any competent knowledge.

But, Sir, I do not think, in the prefent inftance, I am bound to ftate to my Conftituents only, a reafon why I vote contrary to their fentiments—I owe it to this Committee—I owe it to *my Country*, to lay before them the reafons why I differ from Gentlemen who have fo earneftly, and fo repeatedly preffed forward to abolifh and abandon a Trade, which, however great their knowledge and abilities may be, hath been formerly approved and encouraged by men, and by Minfters, who have heretofore fat in this Houfe, whofe humanity, whofe *philanthropy*, and whofe regard for Juftice have equalled thofe of the Honourable Mover, or any of the Supporters of this Propofition ; and whofe abilities were as fplendid as any of the Honourable or Right Honourable Gentlemen who have fpoken in this Debate.

I will endeavour, Sir, not to take up the attention of the Committee, in defcanting upon thofe parts of the fubject which have been already

ready fairly and fufficiently elucidated, by the Gentlemen who have fpoken on the fame fide of the queftion with myfelf. The Honourable Gentleman on my right hand * has clearly and fully fhewn the fatal effect this meafure, if adopted, muft in all probability have on the manufactures, the commerce, and the naviga-tion of this kingdom. The whole body of Evidence upon your Table fufficiently con-tradicts the fabulous accounts of the cruelty exercifed over the Negroes in the Weft-Indies : nor ought the teftimony of Mr. Hercules Rofs, the Wharfinger, to whom Negroes who had been guilty of crimes were fent, from all parts of the town of Kingfton and the neighbour-hood, to receive the punifhment due to their demerits, to be regarded in proof of fevere treatment, when fuch treatment is denied by fo many irreproachable Witneffes, who have teftified the contrary.—There is, indeed, a very ftrong objection to Mr. Rofs's Evidence— an objection which I pledge myfelf, if necef-fary, to prove to be founded in truth. To make himfelf appear of more confequence, and

* Mr. Baillie.

to

to merit the attention of the Committee of
this Houfe, before whom he was examined,
he has declared, " that he has often had the
" honour of accompanying both Governors
" and Admirals *upon tours* in the Ifland of Ja-
" maica." I am authorifed to fay, by fome
of the moft refpectable Gentlemen of the
Ifland, now in London, that this declaration
is *not true*, and that they never knew him to
accompany any Governor or Admiral upon
fuch tours, except Sir Archibald Campbell,
upon *duty* as a *Militia Officer* ; he went with
him to St. Thomas's in the Eaft, and afterwards into another parifh : but this man never
was a companion of, or on equal footing with
men of rank, notwithftanding by Privateering,
and *other modes* nearly as honourable, he acquired a confiderable fortune in the courfe of
laft War. This Gentleman's account, however, is thought the fitteft to contraft with
that of *fifteen* Governors and Admirals, whofe
Evidence lies on your Table ; to fay nothing
of the teftimonies of as many of the moft
refpectable inhabitants, and of the Legiflative
Bodies of the feveral Iflands of the Weft-Indies

dies, who give accounts of the treatment of Slaves, directly contrary to thofe of Mr. Rofs.

Forgive me, Sir, if my zeal for the Truth has made me deviate from my propofed plan, which was to fpeak to the nature of the Trade in Africa, and leave the treatment of the Negroes in the Weft Indies to the confideration of the Committee, upon the Evidence on your Table, which, notwithftanding what has been advanced by an Honourable Gentleman to the contrary, I cannot conceive any Member to be unacquainted with.

Sir, I have read that part of the Evidence on your Table, refpecting the manner in which Slaves are purchafed in Africa, with particular attention ; and I muft own I fee things in a very different point of view from that in which they feem to have appeared to the Right Honourable Gentlemen, whofe abilities have been fo defervedly fubjects of eulogium this night. Thofe Gentlemen have afferted, that none of the Honourable Gentlemen who are their Opponents have ventured to deny, " That the " only

" only modes by which Slaves are obtained
" in Africa, are by their being kidnapped or
" taken in wars, made for that fole purpofe;
" or being condemned for crimes real or
" imaginary: and they call upon any of the
" Supporters of the Slave Trade to fhew how
" otherwife they are obtained?"

Sir, it is certainly a difficult and an unplea-
fant tafk for any Member of this Committee to
encounter the arguments urged by Gentlemen,
whofe oratorical talents have enabled them to
give additional weight to their opinions, by
the forcible manner in which they have delivered them. But, Sir, facts are fuch ftub-
born things, that I hope the plain manner in
which I fhall lay them before the Committee
will not fo far prevent their being attended to,
as to injure the caufe I am endeavouring to
defend. I lament I am not poffeffed of abilities equal to thofe of my Opponents, to
enable me to place the facts I am about to
ftate in the manner they deferve to be preffed
on your attention.

I flatter

I flatter myself, however, that I have it in my power to shew to the Committee, that the Honourable and Right Honourable Gentlemen, who have given so frightful an account of the conduct of the persons trading to Africa, have totally mis-stated the manner in which that Trade is carried on: and that wars are never made for the purpose of obtaining Slaves; and that kidnapping is neither allowed of, nor practised, from one end of the Coast to the other.

The truth of my assertion, and of those of my Opponents, must depend upon such Testimonies as lie upon your table, and the Histories of Africa *formerly* written.—The sources of our information are the same; and it may seem extraordinary, that Gentlemen should draw such different conclusions from the same premises. But, Sir, every Member of this House must allow that *kidnapping* is not an African word—as an English one, I believe the import of it is *stealing young children.* But do we know what is the meaning of the African words of which it is considered a *translation?* I have

the

the same observation to make as to the signifi-
cation of the word *war*. Igno ant of the several
African words, I can only collect their meaning
from the manner in which the English words
are applied ; and that I may not be supposed to
be partial in my account of such application, I
shall confine myself in a great measure to the
account given by the Witnesses examined in
support of the opinion of the Gentlemen who
favour the idea of the Abolition of the Trade,

Sir, some of the Witnesses speak of wars and
kidnapping as the means of procuring Slaves ;
while others, much more likely to know, assert
that wars put a stop to such Trade : and that
kidnapping or stealing men with impunity is *im-
practicable.*—If the persons who give these different accounts are in any degree worthy of
credit, they must by the same words mean something very different. To fix, therefore, the sense
in which these words are understood by the natives on the coast, is the task I have proposed to
myself ; and I hope in performing it I shall con-
vince the Committee, " That it is clear, from

" the

" the Evidence of both parties, that *wars are not*
" *entered into for the purpose of procuring Slaves* ;
" *and that men are not, nor can be stolen with*
" *impunity, either by the Traders, or the persons*
" *of whom they purchase Slaves.*"

The Gentlemen who have asserted these practices in the most positive terms, and to whose
evidence I am willing to allow every degree of
credit, are General Rooke and Captain Wilson.
It is upon the Evidence of these Gentlemen I
rely in proof of my assertion.

The General was two months and ten days on
the Island of Goree; " he never knew him-
" self that the King of Damel pillages his own
" villages ; but *he has understood* that when he
" wanted Slaves, he made *war* for the purpose of
" obtaining them : he never saw any wounded
" people brought in from the villages that
" had been broken up by the King of Damel's
" *troops.*". He says, " kidnapping was spoken of as a common practice." But it does not

appear

appear the General had any knowledge of the language of the country, any more than Mr. Wadstrom : and the next Witness, Captain Wilson, informs the Committee that Alcades and petty Magistrates are distributed in every village, to receive the dues for their Kings ; and that they seem very regular and exact in collecting and demanding them.

He saw one instance of a free man brought for sale by the King of Damel's Guards, which he gives as an instance of kidnapping; but it appears afterwards, by his own testimony, that this man was condemned for setting a corn field belonging to the King on fire.

The General indeed, mentions a *proposition* made to him, to send 100, or 150 of the natives on board the merchant ships which were there, *as Slaves*. He mentions also, that four or five of the King of Damel's subjects went on board one of the merchant ships, who, upon application to him, were brought on shore, and sent to the King

by

by his Maraboo. The Captain of the merchant
ship said, " he kept them on board because
they were drunk :" and surely we cannot doubt
that fact, for there is not the least reason to suppose there was any intention of keeping them
on board, with intent to carry them away, or that
these merchant ships were there *trading for Slaves.*
Upon this principle we may conclude also, that
what the Hon. Member calls *a proposition*, could
be no more than a vague *conversation* ; and such
it appears to have been, from the General's own
account. It happened in public, when the General was upon the parade, attending the troops,
and in presence of the *Maraboos*, who were the
King of Damel's Officers. In the course of the
conversation on *this proposition*, the Masters of the
merchantmen said, *it* had been done by a former
Governor ; but the *Maraboos*, upon being asked,
said. " they did not recollect that any *English*
" Governor had complied with the *request.*"

If this had been any thing more than a vague
conversation, which the General recalls to his recollection at the end of eleven years, would he
have

have taken so little notice of the matter, as not to remember who were the *Masters* of the vessels by whom such a *proposition* was made, or the names of the ships?

Would he at the time have mentioned it to the King of Damel's Officers? Would he not have informed himself whether, if no *English* Governor had ever consented to such a request, any *French* Governor had ever done so? Is it possible he should not at the time (though probably after so long an interval he remembers little about it) have reflected, such an atrocious act would have brought on a war with the Damel, and put a stop to all that intercourse with the main land, which could not be carried on without that King's leave? and without which, the General tells us, his garrison could neither have been supplied with fresh provisions nor water.

But, in proof that there was nothing *serious* in this proposition, and that the ships were not at Goree for the purpose of buying Slaves, it appears from the General's account, that the

King

King offered to sell twenty Slaves within three days, if the English Merchants would give him the price he asked, [twenty pounds] but it seems none were bought. The ships, therefore, were not there to purchase Slaves.

The enormities said to be committed at Senegal and Goree, by Captain Wilson and Mr. Wadstrom, were exercised by the French; and if the Evidence of these Gentlemen proves any thing, it is, that the English *did not* make use of such infamous modes to procure Slaves, and that the French *did.*

But a more close inquiry will shew that they were used neither by one nor the other. *John Barnes,* Esq. Governor of Senegal, while under the English dominion, and *Thomas Poplet,* Esq. an Officer in the Army, who remained there several years, have testified, that no such practices ever take place; that *wars* are *never* made for the purposes of procuring Slaves; and that such kidnapping is even *impossible.* I am ready to allow that the King of Damel, and other Princes between the

the Senegal and Gambia, do cause their villages
to be *brokenup*, and their subjects to be *seized*.
But there is so evident and reasonable a way of re-
conciling these apparently different accounts of
the Witnesses upon this business, that I am astonished it should not strike the generality of the
Members of this Committee; though I am not
surprised, that Gentlemen who seek for nothing
but cruelty, war, and murder, should have over-
looked it.

Sir, it appears, both from the Evidence of the
General and Captain Wilson, that there were regular duties or customs in the King of Damel's
dominions; and Captain Wilson *has heard*, that
the King's Officers had seized the boats and men
who had refused to pay them. If Captain
Wilson had called this seizure of the boats and
men by the appellation of *kidnapping*, it would
have helped us to a right understanding of what
is meant by *that term*; for, it is plain, from the
whole of the Evidence reported to the House on
the 4th of May, 1790, (now upon your Table)
that this breaking up of villages, and kidnapping,

ping, were legal modes of procedure for recovering the *taxes or customs in arrear*, or the debts due to the King or to individuals; which I do not recollect to have been the case in any other part of the country.

You will observe, Sir, that regular annual taxes are payable in these countries, and customs by ships coming to trade. When these taxes and customs are in arrear or due, there must be some mode of collecting them. This mode appears to be by the King's sending his Guards to collect them. We are told by Mr. Poplet, in his Evidence,* delivered before the Privy Council, "that in such case, notice is given that the payment must be made by a certain day: in case of failure the village is broken up; that is, the King's Soldiers surround the village, and catch as many of the inhabitants as they can. They are sold for Slaves, if they do not redeem themselves by the payment of such taxes or duties: if they do, they are released." In like manner, the parties who owe particular sums, either to the King or private persons, or have committed offences,

which

* Report of the Committee of Privy Council, p. 11.

which subject the offenders to punishment, are seized, and become the property of those to whom they owe the money, or against whom the offences have been committed. Captain Poplet, who was a King's Officer, says expressly, the King never breaks a village but upon such occasion. The first of these expeditions the English Traders call *war, or pillage;* the second they have called *kidnapping.*

Give me leave to suppose, Sir, that any of the Gentlemen who have so *eloquently* descanted on the cruelty of this mode of proceeding, (who know no more of the language of the Damel, than the Gentlemen who have told us that *wars* and *kidnapping* are the means of obtaining Slaves) should be examined by one of the King of Damel's *Maraboos* upon this subject—I will beg leave to suppose it should be *the Right Honourable Gentleman* * who has just spoken; he certainly knows better than any body how taxes are collected in this country—Suppose the Maraboo should ask him how the King of Great Britain collected the duties on *Brandy,* for instance, a

D   com-

* Mr. Pitt.

commodity the people in Africa are well acquainted with ; and the Maraboo should be told that
every man who brought any into this country, should be obliged to pay *a bar*, or *a bar and
a half* for every gallon he should import—the Maraboo would naturally consider such duty so hea-
vy, as to render it very difficult to pay; and
would ask how it was collected from the *impor-
ter*, when he endeavoured to avoid the payment, by importing it clandestinely ? and the
Right Honourable Gentleman was to describe the
manner of sending *soldiers* on shore, or *ships* or
cutters at sea, after the *smugglers*—would not
the Maraboo conclude, that the King of G eat
Britain *made war* upon his *subjects*, in order to
compel the payment of such *duties ?* If the Right
Hon. Gentleman was to describe the manner in
which a particular person was *arrested* for non-
payment of any money due to the Crown, upon
process issuing from the Court of Exchequer,
could he do it otherwise than by describing to
the Maraboo how the debtor was seized and imprisoned ? Ccould he use any other English word
to make himself understood but *kidnapped*, or the
African word so translated, in *Senegambia ?* I believe,

lieve, no man who attentively considers the account given by the Evidences examined before the Privy Council and the Committee of this House, respecting *these wars*, and *this kidnapping*, but will be ready to say to him : " *mutato nomine, de te fabula narratur.*" In one particular, indeed, it would be difficult for the Honourable Gentleman to make himself understood by the Maraboo : so far as the *wars*, or the *arrest* or *kidnapping* of the *debtor*, all would go well—but when the Maraboo should ask what was done in England with the *kidnapped person ?* and he should be told he is sent to confinement, the Maraboo would naturally ask if he is put in the *slave hole*, or *captiverie*, (as Mr. Wadstrom calls it.) But he would hardly believe that no Traders ever came to purchase him ; and that the poor *(kidnapped)* white man was kept there for ever, and not *humanely* put to death, as is the case in Africa, when no purchaser offers, instead of being *perpetually* imprisoned.

I dare say, Sir, that the Committee will agree in the justice of my remarks ; and be satisfied, that by putting the construction I have done, on

the

the *wars* and *kidnapping* mentioned by the Evidences who have spoken of the customs of the inhabitants of the country between the Senegal and the Gambia, the different accounts given by the Gentlemen whose Evidence is on your Table, are perfectly reconcileable, and are both consistent and probable; and that *wars, for the purpose of making Slaves, are not made, nor is kidnapping a custom in Africa.*

The Honourable Mover of this question of the Abolition, and his Right Honourable Friends, call upon the Favourers of this Trade, which they describe as so horrid, so cruel, and so infamous, to shew them from whence these thousands of Slaves come, which are annually transported to America. I have shewn from whence they do not come. They do not come from *wars* or *kidnapping.* Sir, I never was concerned in the Slave Trade, and therefore I might, without a blush, confess my ignorance of that matter; but, Sir, on a subject of so much importance, I have thought it my duty to make all the inquiry in my power. I find, as well by the Evidence taken before the Committee of the Privy Council, eil, as before the Committee of this House, that they are brought from a vast distance for sale; that they are bred for that purpose : and the *worthy* Itinerant Clergyman, whose labours, in promoting the view of the Abolitionists, has been so *justly* praised by the Honourable Gentleman who has brought forward this question, tells us, in his Essay on Slavery, p. 122, 123, "They come from *the great mountains*, through *barren sands* and *inhospitable woods*, at such an *amazing* distance from the coast, that the journey could scarcely be compleated in seven moons." That such Slaves are brought to be sold from a great distance, is clear, from all the antient Histories of Africa. The Slaves sold in the River Senegal, come chiefly from Galam, *nine hundred or one thousand miles* within land. This we learn as well from the Evidence upon our Table, as from the Histories of Africa. Not only the *ingenious* Gentleman, Mr. Moore, whose authority has been quoted to-night by an Honourable Member,* tells us the same thing ; but Smythe, Barbot, Adanson, and Marchais, concur in the same account. Villault tells us, that when he was

* Mr. Thornton.

on the Gold Coast, a war, which continued four years, *entirely put a stop to Trade*. The Directors of the European Slaving Companies did all they could to accommodate matters between the contending parties, to no effect. Captain Phillips also tells us, that *on account of the wars there*, no Slaves could be had on the *Gold Coast*. Marchais says, *on account of the wars* between the Kings of Whidaw and Ardra, no Slaves could be had at the Rio-volta. These accounts, which are all to be found in the several Collections of Voyages, made long before the agitation of this question, are surely convincing proofs, that the Princes of Africa *do not go to war for the purpose of making Slaves:* the Evidence of Captains Penny, Fraser, Governor Dalzel, Mr. Norris, in the volume on your Table, * are full to that point : and Thomas Anderson, Esq. particularly testifies, that *on account of wars* which lasted two years, a Bristol ship was obliged to wait that time, before she could purchase any. These Gentlemen all tell us, that the Slaves are brought very far from the interior of the country. Surely, the Reverend Gentleman before men-

* Evidence before the Committee of Privy Council p. 9. & seq.

mentioned, will meet with credit from the Honourable and Right Honourable Gentlemen who have supported the Abolition. They will probably excuse the *zeal* with which he has *exaggerated* the length of their march, but if it continued three instead of seven moons, was it not a fair and accustomed Trade to bring down such Slaves to market ? But were the accounts of wars and kidnapping to be taken in the sense those words have been used in this Committee, the persons who set out with them would never arrive at the coast. If *thousands* of Slave-Merchants, as this Reverend Gentleman tells us, travel a thousand miles to entrap and *kidnap* the unwary, * would it be possible these *kidnapped* people should be suffered to pass through those countries, which the Honourable Gentleman tell us, are civilized people, to the coast, where the inhabitants have learned inhumanity from their commerce with the Europeans ? This surely is sufficient to prove, that a very small part only of the Negroes purchased by the Traders are *prisoners of war*, or what has been called *kidnapped*; and the latter will appear to be persons

* Clarkson's Essay, p. 75.

sons who have not paid their taxes, have defraud-
ed their creditors, or have committed some crimes
for which they have been condemned by the Ju-
dicature of the Country.

I hope, Sir, what I have said upon this subject
will satisfy the Right Honourable Gentleman*
who called on the Friends of the Slave Trade to
shew how Slaves are obtained; without having
recourse *to war, to kidnapping, to fraud, or vio-
lence.*

I cannot, Sir, help observing, that the Honourable Member who has provoked this discussion, has painted the situation of the Slaves in
the West Indies as unhappy and miserable; and
that, notwithstanding the testimony of the Gentlemen, whose names have before been mentioned to-night, to the contrary: Rodney, Bar-
rington, Hotham, Shuldham, Dalling, Campbell, and other Gentlemen, who are an honour
to their Country and to human nature. These
Gentlemen tell you the condition of the Slaves
in the West Indies is superior to that of the

Poor

* Mr. Fox.

Poor in this country. The Honourable Mover of this question has told us, he has not any intention of emancipating the Slaves in the West Indies; why then state their condition as unhappy? Why charge the West India Gentlemen with treating their Slaves with cruelty? Why complain, that the Negroes are deprived of legal protection, and, by his misrepresentation of the situation of these people, endeavour to make them as unhappy as he paints them? Can such declarations answer any purpose but to stir up a revolt? The Honourable Gentleman, Sir, tells us, he has enquired into the circumstances which led to the horrid massacres, and other dreadful mischiefs, which have happened at Saint Domingo. He has satisfied himself, that they have not arisen from the proceedings of himself and his Friends in the Old Jewry. It is happy for *him*, and *them*, if they can so persuade themselves; they must otherwise be *miserable* as long as they exist. I should certainly be so, if I was one of them; for I also have made the strictest enquiry into this business, and I have no doubt, not only that that insurrection, and those in our

E   Islands,

Islands, which have happily been suppressed, have originated from the writings and proceedings of these Gentlemen; but that it is from thence, and from the successful endeavours of their *Reverend* Ambassador to the *Jacobines* at Paris,* that the decrees have passed the National Assembly, which have occasioned the disputes between the White Men and the People of Colour in that Island. The insurrection of the Negroes is attributed, by the Deputies of St. Domingo, to the Society which sprung up in the bosom of France, but which originated from Foreigners. What *Foreigners* could it have originated from, but the Honourable Gentleman's Friends? It is said by them, to be owing to the wishes expressed by the Abbé Gregoire, " that the sun might soon shine on none but Freemen ;" (an expression similar to that of the Hon. Gentleman, † who has declared his wish, " that the day might soon arrive when all *mankind* may enjoy the *blessings* of liberty")—to the expression of a *French Patriot*, ‡ who declared his wishes, " that the Colonies might perish, rather than the principles of the Rights of Man be infringed"—

a wish

* Mr. Clarkson.   † Mr. Thornton.   ‡ Mr. Roberspierre.

a wish not very dissimilar from that of a Right Honourable Gentleman * on the other side of the House, respecting the Colonies of this Country : and there are too many reasons to dread such declarations will be attended with similar effects in our Colonies.

Sir, the Honourable Mover of this question professes much kindness to the West India Planters. It is for *their sakes* he would prevent a further importation of Negroes. I believe the Planters do not desire his favours. There is not one of them who is not ready to say—

"" Timeo Danaos, et dona ferentes.""

Had the Honourable Gentleman, or the Right Honourable and Honourable Gentlemen who supported his motion for the Abolition of the Slave Trade, entered into a fair discussion of it, had they stated the Evidence on both sides with impartiality, I am convinced there is not a Gentleman who would have complained. I am sure, Sir, I would not have troubled the Committee upon this occasion. But when I hear the Gen-

E 2   tlemen

* Mr. 𝕏 𝕠𝕥.

tlemen of the other side call upon the House to support their attempt to abolish the Trade, because the voice of the People demand it, I cannot help being astonished. I can no longer consider the Gentlemen as acting from motives of Justice or Humanity. An Hon. Gentleman* on the other side of the House has exposed to the Committee the mode in which the supposed sense of the People has been obtained. Gentlemen, in addition to what my Honourable Friend read to you on that subject, I have in my hand, a Letter from a very respectable Gentleman in Edinburgh, in which I am informed the *Reverend* Gentleman who has been alluded to before, visited Edinburgh, Glasgow, Paisley, &c. to obtain Signatures to the Petition from the former place. The Provost and Magistrates of Edinburgh, the College of Physicians, and the Members of the University, were too well informed, to be prevailed on. I believe, you will not find ten Gentlemen of Character have put their names to the Petition: Sectaries, Porters, Scavengers, and School-Boys, will be found to make up ninetenths of the people whose names appear to it ;

and

* Colonel Tarleton.

and half the remainder will be found absolutely fictitious. But, Sir, it is not merely this mode of personally soliciting Petitions, that I repro- bate : Sir, by far the greatest part of the Pe- titions were from places, where hardly any of the inhabitants can be supposed competent to judge upon the subject, even if they had the Evidence respecting it before them : but, Sir, such Petitions as have been obtained fr n them, appear to have been obtained by false representa- tions of the purport of that Evidence ; by garbled and partial accounts of it. Can Gentlemen boast of a regard for Humanity, or be guided by a love of Justice, who have been guilty of such practices—I had almost said *infamous* practices ! But I refrain from using that epithet, from having heard a Right Honourable Gentleman, * whose integrity I *used* to think equal to his splendid abilities, avow himself *one* of the Com- mittee of the *Society* in the *Old Jewry*, who ad- vised the distribution of such accounts, which have tended so to deceive and impose upon the people of this country. The Right Honourable Gentleman has ironically said, the West-India Planters

---

* Mr. Fox.

Planters might have behaved in a similar manner, unless they are supposed to be *too virtuous*
to have taken such steps. I have the happiness,
Sir, to be much acquainted with the West-India
Gentlemen, and, notwithstanding the sneer of
the Right Honourable Gentleman, I am bold to
say, that I do not believe they would have taken
the same *unfair means* of imposing on the cre-
dulity of the people of this country, if it would
have obtained the *unanimous* voice of this Committee, in *rejection* of the motion at present before us.

This avowal of the means by which the Petitions on your Table have been obtained, has
not more amazed than grieved me. It makes
me apprehensive that *some* of the Gentlemen
who support the Honourable Mover of this question, have much more *extensive views* than the
bare Abolition of the Slave Trade. When I find
this question supported by the Heads of the
Sectaries in different parts of the kingdom—
when I learn that they preach against this Trade,
and spread abroad *false accounts* of the mode of

its

its being carried on, and hoi.d *themselves* forth as the just and humane men who solicit the suppression of it—when I see *such* a correspondence settled between Clubs and Societies established in London, and the remotest *villages* in the kingdom—I cannot help turning my view to a neighbouring nation, where the *same kind of correspondence* has overturned the Government of the finest country in Europe, and deluged it in blood and slaughter. How soon may we expect a similar fate, if similar proceedings are not put a stop to? If the Resolutions of this Committee, or of this House, are to be governed by the Resolutions of *Societies* similar to those of France; or of Petitions or Addresses obtained by the means of such *misrepresentations* as these Societies shall spread abroad, among those with whom, in the language of the *Club of the Jacobines*, they shall be *affiliated?*

A Right Hon. Gentleman, * whose weight with the House is deservedly great, and whose abilities and eloquence are sufficient *to make the worse appear the better cause*, has exerted both

in

* Mr. Pitt.

in support of the motion. He has endeavoured to shew, that the Abolition of this Trade cannot be injurious to our West-India Colonies, " be-
" cause it appears we are able now to keep up the
" present stock by the number of births, which,
" upon an average in all the Islands, equal, if they
" do not exceed the deaths." But permit me to observe to this Committee, that if there be already a sufficient number of Negroes in our Colonies, this argument proves too much—there would be no need to *abolish* a Trade which would end of itself, because there would be no market for the Slaves in the West Indies, and consequently no person would bring them over. If we have at present not a sufficient number, it proves nothing. The consequences of not procuring more would most probably be, that the births would again become less in number than the deaths: and the Right Hon. Gentleman should consider, that, even if the births and deaths should continue equal, the loss of a full-grown Slave could not be repaired under *eighteen* or *twenty* years. The example the Right Hon. Gentleman produces, from the testimony of one

of

of the Legislative Bodies, * that a free Negro
will do as much work in two hours as a Slave
will do in ten, would be conclusive, so far as to
induce the Planter to wish all his Slaves free,
provided he knew how to compel or induce them
to work afterwards longer than the two hours
necessary for their own purposes. But I hope,
Sir, I may be allowed also to say, that notwithstanding what the Honourable Mover and his
Friends assert, respecting the severity of the labour of the Slaves in the West-Indies, the example
the Right Hon. Gentleman cites, is a proof, that in
the nine or ten hours in which the Negroes work
for their Masters, they do not do more than a
fifth part of the work they might do, if they
chose to labour for their Masters as for themselves. At any rate, it is a proof, that whatever
instances of severity are urged against the Owners
of Negroes, that of *severe labour* is not among
the number.

The Right Honourable Gentleman spoke with
contempt of the just apprehension which an Honourable Gentleman on his left hand had expressed, † that foreign nations would extend the

F   Trade

---

* The Council and Assembly of Jamaica.
† The Honourable Mr. Jenkinson.

Trade in proportion as this country relinquished it. He desires to know, where are the Merchants—where the capital with which to carry on such a commerce? Might not Louis the Fourteenth have asked the same question as to the manufacture of Silk, when he revoked the Edict of Nantes? Sir, I will tell the Right Hon. Gentleman where the Merchants and where the capital will be found. Sir, our own Merchants will establish themselves in Havre, Bourdeaux, Nantes, Dunkirk, Ostend, Copenhagen, and other places; and they will take their capitals, their ships, and their skill with them, from London, Liverpool, Bristol, and Lancaster; and it is more than probable, the manufacturers of Manchester and Birmingham will follow them. I say *Copenhagen*, because, notwithstanding what has fallen from the Right Hon. Gentleman on the Treasury Bench, the King of Denmark has no idea of abolishing the Slave Trade, till there are as many Negroes in his Sugar Colonies as are fully sufficient for their cultivation;* and Denmark, as

well

* The Edict of the King of Denmark has since been printed, whereby it appears, that in order to encourage the Trade the *Philanthropists* of this country wish to abolish, he allows his subjects to export Sugar even in foreign bottoms, and to any country they think proper, in order to pay for them: he also lends the Planters in St. Cruz money at four per cent. interest, that they may be enabled to purchase them.

well as Spain, encourages your Merchants to
supply their Colonies. Sir, the proposition of
the Hon. Gentleman to whom I last alluded, *
(whose knowledge and abilities, at so early a period of life, afford the most pleasing prospect
to his country of what may be expected from
him, when those abilities shall be matured, and
that knowledge increased by experience) appears
to me to be fraught with the knowledge of commerce and mankind; he has suggested the dif-
ficulty there will be in preventing Foreigners
from supplying your Sugar Islands with Negroes, even should an Act pass here to abolish
the Slave Trade. It is with no less surprize than
concern I heard a Right Hon. Gentleman †
inform the Committee of the means he conceived
he had in his power to prevent such supply :—
he tells us, the King appoints the Governors,
the Officers of the Revenue, and the Judges of
the Courts of Justice. You have, he tells you,
your Navy, with which the Islands in the West
Indies may be, as it were, surrounded; and you
may therefore command the Trade of the Colonies. Thus you are taught to think that the
same attempt, which you in vain sought to ex-

F 2   ecute

* The Honourable Mr. Jenkinson.   † Mr. Pitt.

ecute at Boston, and which lost your American
Colonies, may be successfully renewed in the
West-Indies. I fancy, however, it will be found,
that a *Kingston Port Act* will not be more effica-
cious than that by which the Port of Boston was
attempted to be *blocked up*.

I have too good an opinion of the Right Honourable Gentleman, to think such sentiments
are the result of his serious reflection ; or that he
will not acknowlege the observations of the Right
Hon. Gentleman opposite to him, * are so just as
to make him abandon the idea of forcing the Colonies, by his threats, to make such laws as shall
be recommended to them from this country. Sir,
it cannot be doubted, the power of this Country
can ruin the Colonies ; but I fancy, neither the
mandates of a Minister, the vigilance of the Officers of Revenue, unjust and time-serving Judges,
if such can be found, or the authority of their
Governors, will make them *tamely* surrender
the rights of *British subjects* without a *struggle*.
You may certainly regulate your own commerce ;
you may say, your own subjects shall not trade to
Africa from Great Britain; you may say, your own
ships shall not carry Negroes to the Colonies; you

may

* Mr. Fox.

may refuse to accept their commodities, and abandon *one third* of your *commerce* and your *revenue* :
but you have no right to say, what shall be the
state of the Negroes in the Colonies : you have no
more right to make laws for the internal regulation of the Negroes in the Colonies, than the Colonies have to regulate your conduct respecting
the management of your Poor You have encouraged these Gentlemen to *purchase* their lands of
Government ; you have even encouraged them to
invest *their fortunes* in the cultivation of them ;
you have encouraged not only *your Merchants*,
but *Foreigners*,* to advance them money for the
purpose of such cultivation. If you now put a
stop to the cultivation, they have a right to come
on you for indemnification.

The Hon. Gentleman I have just alluded to,‡
has shewn you, Sir, in the clearest manner, that
the cause of Humanity will suffer by the attempt to abolish the Slave Trade. Under the
regulations you have made, the mortality in the
Middle Passage is now reduced to less than three
per cent. Additional regulations or experience
may render it still less. It is, however, at present
less than the mortality on board the transport
ships.

* Act of 14th Geo. III. ‡ The Hon. Mr. Jenkinson.

ships. I have strong reasons, however, to
fear the purposes of Humanity have been less advanced by these regulations than this Committee
can imagine ; some *facts* have come to my knowledge which show the contrary ; * and prove the
propriety of not suffering children at the breast,
to be accounted as one of the number of those
who are permitted to be carried in proportion
to the tonnage of the vessel.

A Right Honourable Gentleman tells us the
reason of the mortality on board *the latter* was
owing to the Master of the transport having before been employed in the Slave Trade. I have
to ask, why employ such a man ? at least, why
did you not make his profit depend on the care
which he took of the people he carried ? That is
the case in the Slave Ships. If the Captain of the

ship

---

* A Captain of a trading ship had a young woman with a child at
her breast brought to him to purchase, which he refused, as by the
late regulation such child would be reckoned among the number he
was permitted to carry.   Some few days after, one of his Officers
purchased a young woman, who having a breast full of milk, and
appearing melancholy, the Captain endeavoured, by his Linguist,
to learn the cause; he found that this poor woman was the same
he had refused some little time before   Her Owner had taken her
away, murdered the infant, and brought her back without the
child.   The *gentle* Abolitionists may glory in their humanity.——
The *barbarous* Slave Captain told the story with the most lively
sentiments of regret.

If this horrid transaction happened in consequence of Regulation, and many others of the same sort will undoubtedly happen,
which we shall know nothing of, the consequences of Abolition will
be a thousand times worse ; in proof of which we refer to the
Histories of Africa, the Evidence on your Table, and the Affida-
vit annexed.

ship does not carry his Slaves safe to market, his profits are proportionably diminished : but I am told the Master of the transport was to have *eighteen pounds* per head for the Convicts he carried, whether they lived or *died* ; which certainly was not calculated to induce him to take more than *ordinary care* of their health.

Sir, the jaundiced eye gives every thing it beholds a yellow tint. We may therefore suppose the Gentlemen who call themselves Abolitionists, have not seen every thing in its proper and natural colour; but when a Right Honourable Gentleman, who seems to be one of the *heads* of the party ; who calls himself the *Man* of the People ; avows intentional misrepresentation; we ought to be particularly attentive to what is advanced from that quarter. The Honourable Gentleman who made the motion before you, has endeavoured to interest the *passions* of the Committee and not their *judgments.* He tells you the Negroes are driven in the field, and whipped like cattle, and are often branded and used with extreme cruelty. There are many Country Gentlemen in the House who have seen their cattle worked in the fields here, who will tell us that the Waggoner or Ploughman generally

rally finds the crack of the whip sufficient for all his purposes. They will tell you, their cattle are *branded* too. This is a step not arising from cruelty, but to prevent the cattle from being *stolen* : why will they suppose any other reason for the Planters marking their *new Negroes,* who cannot tell their Owners names ?

When the *executioners* were murdering *Don Carlos,* the Infant of Spain, they told him *it was all for his good.* The Gentlemen who are for destroying the Planters tell us the same. They quote Mr. Long, to shew us that in 1775 the Planters were fearful of importing Negroes from a particular part of Africa ; the persons so imported were rebellious, and had been the authors of sundry insurrections. * These Negroes were generally called Cormantees. Mr. Long did not then know why these Negroes were more turbulent than others. A further knowledge of the country and its history has since informed us, they were really prisoners of war. There was a little before that period a war between the King of Ashantee and Akim ; a number of both

were,

---

* Mr. Long also observed, that the number of Negroes then imported were three times as many as in former years; and therefore thought, with reason, the number of new Negroes too many to be imported at once, in proportion to the Creole Negroes on the Island ; a reason which no longer exists.

were, contrary to the *common custom* of the country, sold to the people of Fantin, instead of being *murdered.* The Planters, as soon as they knew who these people were, refused to purchase them : they even in 1774 framed a law, laying a duty on the importation of Negroes above certain ages, which was rejected by the King in Council, as injurious to that commerce, which they now wish to destroy.

Sir, it has been judiciously observed by a Right Honourable Gentleman,* that before the late regulations, the Merchants concerned in the Trade to Africa, complained that their commerce would be ruined, if *these regulations* took place. They now, however, find their profits have increased. *The Planters*, says the Right Honourable Gentleman, will, perhaps, find that the Abolition will be *advantageous* to them. But if the Right Hon. Gentleman will seek the reason why the prediction of the African Merchants is not verified, he will find that they have saved themselves, by *raising the price* of the Slaves on the Planter twenty-five per cent. and the Planter, by having, for two years past, found the price of all the produce of his lands in-

G

creased,

* Mr. Dundas.

creased, has been enabled to give *such advanced price* without being ruined.

Measures, Sir, however, are now taking, which will deprive the Planter of that advantage. I am told the Right Honourable Gentleman means to prevent *Sugar* in particular, from continuing at a high price.—Instead of waiting the regular diminution of the price, from an *increase of produce*, which is always the consequence of a scarcity, we are told " we will deprive you of the means of increasing your cultivation; but you shall sell us the commodity cheaper than heretofore." Thus said the Egyptian Task-masters of old—" There shall no straw be given you, yet shall ye deliver the tale of bricks as heretofore." Sir, I am sorry to be obliged to observe, that every species of misinformation and misrepresentation, which ingenuity can furnish, or invent, is given to this Committee. It has appeared in Evidence, as well before this House as before the Committee of Privy Council, and it his evident from all the histories of Africa, that *human sacrifices* are much diminished on the coast ; and the people are in some degree civilized by their intercourse with the Europeans ;

but

but that such *sacrifices* still exist in the interior part of the country. To induce you to discredit these circumstances, you are told, that every thing is now *savage* on the *coast*, and that the *interior* of the country is *civilized.* You are told, Sir, of savage acts of barbarity committed by Captains of slave ships, and the account of the *murders* and *sacrifices* of the natives by their *Princes* is diminished to an isolated fact, of a Negro man's hanging his young Slave, who had run away from him three times, in Africa. Instead of the man thus riddig himself of his Slave, by hanging him, the Witness, Captain Fraser, says he was put to death in a most cruel manner: " his Master began, by cutting off his *hands* at his wrists, then his *arms* at his elbows, and then the *stumps* from his shoulders ; he afterwards began to cut off the *feet* at the ancles ; the rest of the joints, and finished with cutting his head off." By the account of this boy being *merely hanged,* the Hon. Gentleman has sought to withdraw the attention of the Committee from the instances of *horrid African cruelty.* In like manner, the Evidence of Governor Miles, Gov. Weuves, Gov. Dalzel, and Governor Devaynes,

now

now on your Table, as to the *sacrificing the Negroes*, is passed over in silence. The testimony of these Gentlemen on this head is positive. Mr. Norris, of his own knowledge, assures us, that *thousands* are thus *annually sacrificed* in the kingdom of *Dahomy*: that he has seen at the gates of the King's palace, *piles of heads*, like *shot* in an arsenal; and the *heads* of persons *newly put to death*, strewed in the passage to the King's apartment: that in general the persons thus *massacred*, are those *refused* to be purchased. The roof of the palace is decorated with a prodigious number of *human sculls*; and so far is this Prince from making war to obtain Slaves, that the phrase in use, when he is going to war, is, " *the palace wants thatching*."

It is not because our Opponents have an aversion to describe such *bloody scenes*, but to mislead the judgment of the Committee, that they have omitted to paint those horrid *pictures of murders, cruelty, and sacrifices*, which humanity must shudder at, and which must make every Member of the Committee wish the unhappy inhabitants removed from the country where they are practised, to another where their lives are
safe,

safe, and where it appears, from the most respectable Evidence, they are *treated with kindness and humanity.* Give me leave, Sir, to say
that such conduct is equally contrary to *justice*
and *humanity, virtues* to which our *Opponents*
make such *exclusive* claims. Is not, Sir, the *suppression of truth* as unjust as *false suggestions?*
I beg leave to say, we have *proof* that several
of our Opponents are guilty *of both.* But a-
mong other acts of *injustice and cruelty,* may
we not rank that of *accusing people,* and blast-
ing their reputation, without giving them an
opportunity of defending themselves? Such,
Sir, has been the conduct of the Abolitionists.
The Planters and African Merchants have *been
accused* of shameful cruelties, on the representa-
tion of people who appear, on the face of their
accounts, to be *ignorant, prejudiced, or unworthy of credit*; upon the bare relation of such
improbable accounts, *not given upon oath*;
(a circumstance, perhaps, unknown to the
people who have been betrayed into presenting
the Petitions on your Table and which accounts
are contradicted by men of the first character
in the kingdom.) Are the fortunes and reputation

of

of the Planters and Merchants of this kingdom
to be put in hazard ?—I say, Sir, put in hazard,
for whatever the Committee may determine,
there is no doubt, but before any Bill which
may be brought into this House shall pass into
an *Act*, so serious a *branch of the commerce
of this country* will not be destroyed or aban-
doned, without a more solemn and serious
inquiry being made before the other branch of
the Legislature, who will examine persons
upon oath, who are competent to give them information ; and will properly *discriminate* between the *credibility* of the persons testimony
who they shall examine.

I have not said much respecting the impolicy
and impracticability of the measure proposed; nor
shall I enlarge upon them. An Hon. Member, *
who is much better qualified than I am to call
your attention to those points, has shewn you
how much Humanity will suffer by your aban-
doning a commerce to nations over whom you
have no controul, which (under the wise regulations you have already made, and others
which you may make hereafter, if necessary)
will be carried on with every degree of attention

to

* Mr. Jenkinson.

to the health and happiness of the objects of it. That Honourable Gentleman has also pointed out to you the only rational mode by which the Abolition of the Trade can be effected, which is by increasing the *births* in the Islands; and for that purpose, the *importation of Females*.

Before I conclude, permit me, Sir, to reply to what has fallen from the Honourable Mover of this question, with respect to the accusations he has preferred against some Captains of ships in the Slave Trade. Sir, the Honourable Mover *piques himself* upon his regard to *Humanity and Justice*. I am sorry, Sir, to say, in these accusations he has shewn himself actuated neither by one or the other.

Sir, by the *humanity of our laws*, no man is considered as guilty till he is put upon his defence, and legally proved so; yet, Sir, a number of people have been accused of horrid crimes and cruelties, *without any such proof*. This conduct, Sir, is equally *inhuman and unjust*; and if, upon inquiry, the Honourable Gentleman should find that his accusations are *unjust and calumnious*, what recompence can he make to the parties he has injured, who have been *no-*

minally

minally held up to public detestation and abhor-
rence? Sir, when the Honourable Gentleman
made these *horrid* charges, I could not refrain
from feeling those sentiments of indignation
which warped my judgmenr, so far as to incline
me to give my vote against the Trade, where
such cruelties could be practised ; but reflecting
on the *misrepresentations* which have been before made by the *Society of Abolitionists*, I first
doubted of the truth of the accusations; and then
was led to consider that, if true, and *fairly proved,*
they were no more a reason for putting a stop
to the Slave Trade, than the cruelties practised
by a *Brownrigg* is a reason for preventing poor
children being placed out apprentices. But, Sir,
I am free to own, I do not believe the facts as
stated. If true, Sir, what have they to do with
a well regulated Trade? Why are the persons
who have been guilty, not brought to condign
punishment? If your laws are not sufficient to
punish such offenders, shame on your laws !
you ought to amend them. If they are, **why**
are they not executed ? I know, however, the
laws *are* sufficient to punish murders committed
on the high seas. Nothing remains then but to

prove

prove the facts, and punish the guilty persons: indeed, if the persons accused should *now* be put upon their country, I fear they are so far *prejudged*, that I doubt how they have a chance of a fair and candid trial. Unless the facts are fairly proved, I will not, I cannot believe them : and that they are false, I am the more inclined to believe, from the Honourable Gentleman's informing us, that the former Owners of the ships those people commanded continue to employ them.

The Honourable Gentleman, in the same flow of eloquence with which he has affected us this night, by the *horrid tales* of cruelty said to be committed by *Captains of ships in the Slave Trade*, shocked his hearers with accounts of cruelties committed by the same sort of Traders last year : * I allude, Sir, to the story of the war between the Towns of *Old* and *New Callebar*. Upon a full inquiry, the story proved false, and fabricated. This circumstance, I should think, Sir, would have induced the Ho-

H   nourable

---

* There was another story told at the same time, of a child whose feet were put into hot water, to abate the swelling of them. Although the Cook put his finger into the water (without scalding it) and told the barbarous *Slave Captain* the water was too hot, he persisted in putting the child's feet in, and scalded *off its nails*. The *Member* who told this *absurd story* was angry at being *laughed at*.

nourable Gentleman to have *paused a little*, before he had suffered his humanity to have run away with his judgment, and his regard to the first principles of justice.

The Honourable Gentleman ought at least to have obtained and stated something like Evidence, as to the truth of the facts, before he accused individuals of crimes which affect their lives—facts which his statement may prevent a fair investigation of in a Court of Justice, and so far operate on the minds of the persons who may be summoned to try these facts, as to put the accused in a situation which may endanger his life, from the prejudice thus raised against him: and the Right Hon. Gentleman might, perhaps, easily have found such Evidence, if the horrid story of the murder of the woman on the Middle Passage is founded in truth. I believe, Sir, by the *Regulation Bill* of last year, the *Surgeon* of the ship is obliged to give an account, *upon oath*, of the number of deaths, and by what *diseases*, or from what *cause* such deaths have happened, during the voyage. If the Surgeon of the ship has given such account of the treatment of the Negro girl, and of her coming to

her

her death from such cause as stated by the Honourable Gentleman, I cannot conceive you
would have heard a complaint, of Capt. Kimber,
the *accused person*, being *at large* in this kingdom. * I have no doubt but the Magistrates, at
the port where he sold his Slaves, would have
committed him to gaol, and he would have been
tried, and if found *guilty*, would have suffered
the punishment due to his crime.

Sir, I must own I feel it as an act of great
cruelty and injustice, that the *property*, the
lives, and the *reputations* of men, and of Gentlemen, should be affected by tales told by people of every description, not sanctioned by oath
—and that such tales (which, when told by the
relaters of them in their own language, no cool
or dispassionate man could credit) should be *as-
sumed as facts, proved, ascertained, and argued upon*, by Gentlemen of such abilities as the Hon.
Mover and Right Hon. Supporters of the question
before us this night. Equally unjustifiable is it in
the Hon. Gentleman to bring forth stories, by
way of *surprising* this Committee into a vote in

H 2   *con-*

---

* If the *Surgeon* of the ship has formerly given a different account of the child's death, *upon oath*, from that which he now
swears to, whichever account is true, he is guilty of perjury.

consequence of them; when the parties to be *affected* by it in their *properties*, to an immense amount, have no chance of replying to, or contradicting them.

Even while I am speaking, Sir, conviction flashes on my mind, that the stories of what passed in Callebar cannot be true! What, Sir, ships from different ports combining to fire on people, in a populous and defenceless town, on the most frequented part of the Coast, to oblige the natives to sell their Slaves at a lower price than they chose to demand for them! which must not only be a probable means of preventing their obtaining any Slaves at all, but must have stopped all Trade there in future. The fact is so incredible, that I cannot hesitate, Sir, to pronounce it a *shameful calumny*; and I am surprized the Honourable Gentleman * has suffered himself to be deluded into the *belief* of it a moment. +

Sir,

* Mr. Wilberforce.

+ It is now known that the whole of this tale originated from the people of the town having obtained the goods which were brought for trade, under a promise to deliver a number of Slaves at a certain price. They afterwards refused to comply with their bargain, or return the goods: in consequence of which the Captains of the ships ordered some guns to be fired over the town, to intimidate the inhabitants, which had the desired effect; but no person was either killed or wounded.

Sir, I cannot consider the reason given by the Honourable Gentleman ‡ for not prosecuting the persons he supposes to have been guilty of such atrocious crimes, as sufficient to induce the Honourable Gentleman to decline bringing the accused persons to trial—he conceives " they ought not to be punished for crimes which the Trade they are in tempts them to commit"—a Trade which the Legislature of the Country has countenanced, or encouraged. Sir, I cannot suppose such a *plea* would be thought sufficient by the Honourable Gentleman, if advanced by people who *rob their Masters*, in order to purchase or insure *tickets* and *shares of tickets* in the *Lottery*.

For these reasons, Sir, I shall most heartily support the motion of my Honourable Friend,* for the Chairman's leaving the Chair.

Sir, it is clear to me, from every page of history, that the Emancipation of persons in Slavery is not to be accomplished hastily. A Right Honourable Gentleman + observed, that the people of this country were once in the same abject state with the inhabitants of Africa—sold

as

‡ Mr. Wilberforce.   * Mr. Jenkinson.   + Mr. Pitt.

as Slaves, and transported to foreign countries. *Such sale*, indeed, was one of the means of their *civilization :* a few of them perhaps returned to their native country, probably with some degree of information, and knowledge of civilized life. The situation in which the people are now on the Coaſt of Africa, *is such as the natives of these kingdoms were in, one thousand years ago :* some of them were *Slaves* so attached to the soil, that they could not be sold from it : others were absolutely in the diſposal of their Masters. The one were called *Villains regardant* ; the other *Villains in gross.* This, Sir, I say, is nearly the ſituation of the Negroes in Africa : it appears clearly, from the Evidence on your Table, that some of the Slaves *there* are what the Witnesses call *Family Slaves*, whose Masters have no right to dispose of them ; the others they may *sell* as they please. Let any Gentleman recollect, how many hundred years elapsed before the condition of the people were changed, and *Villanage* worn out in this kingdom, after the sale of the inhabitants to foreigners ceaseď ; and he must be convinced of the futility of abolishing such Trade or intercourse with Africa ; and the justice of my

Hon.

Hon. Friend's observations will be evident—that
the only rational mode of abolishing the Slave
Trade, is to increase the population in the West
Indies; and that the mode of doing so, in the
speediest and most effectual manner, is by increasing the importation of young women. When
by that means you have as many Negroes in the
Colonies as you have occasion for, the Trade
to Africa for them will end of course. This
will be a *gradual Abolition*, and the only mode
by which a *gradual* Abolition can take place,
consistent with *Justice or Humanity*. In time,
this will also abolish *Servitude*—for it is an abuse
of the word, to call the condition of the Negroes
in the West-Indies, *Slavery*.

There was an observation made by an Honourable Gentleman upon the floor,* which, I
own, gave me pleasure—it was relative to the
probable advantages that the Negroes in the
West-Indies might reap if the Honourable Member, and the Honourable Mover of the Proposition before the Committee, were to visit the
West-Indies : the Hon. Gentleman seemed to fear
they would not be able to be of any advantage to
those whose lot they deplore. I own I am much

of

* Mr. Smith.

of the same opinion, but perhaps for a *different reason*. From what appears upon the face of the Evidence before us, I do not think their condition stands in any great need of amelioration; but I can tell the Hon. Gentlemen what benefit they will reap from the voyage, especially if they will go round *by Africa*. In the first place, the Hon. Gentleman, * *whose couch is watered with his tears*, and whose sleep is interrupted, from reflecting on the miserable situation and distresses of the people in Africa, in consequence of the horrors committed by the Masters of Slave-ships, and the Slave Trade ; will be restored to his natural rest and peaceful slumbers : and the other Honourable Gentleman † will either be convinced that he and his family may *again* make use of *Sugar*, without considering themselves swallowing the *blood* of those who made it; and with more satisfaction enjoy the wealth which he possesses, and which many people suppose to have been acquired by *dealing* in that very *commodity* ; or he will be convinced of the justice of the opinions he now entertains, and atone for the former *guilt* of *such traffick*, by appropriating the fortune so unjustly obtained to *pious uses*.

* Mr. Wilberforce.　　† Mr. Smith.

FINIS.

APPENDIX.

As it has been afferted, by the perfons who call themfelves The Friends to the Abolition of the Slave-Trade, that fuch Trade is cruel, bloody, and unjuft; and that the Africans are a peaceable and happy people, except when induced to wage war with each other by the Europeans : As the Gentlemen who have fet themfelves againft this Traffick, have felected from the evidence *brought* before the Committee of the Houfe laft year fuch accounts as beft anfwered their purpofe, of inducing a belief that fuch enormities are committed as make the putting a ftop to that Commerce an act of juftice : And as the Weft India Planters and African Merchants have an-tagonifts who are capable of mifreprefenting facts

H   in

in such a manner as to dazzle and mislead their hearers, they trust in the justice and impartiality of the Members of the House of Commons, to refer to the testimony of the Gentlemen who appeared before the Committee of the Privy Council, which it is impossible they can read with attention without being convinced.

I. That wars in Africa are never entered into for the purpose of making prisoners to sell to the Europeans.

II. That the parts of the country where the Europeans trade have made confiderable approaches to civilization.

III. That the Negroes who are within reach of a Commercial Intercourse with the inhabitants of the Coast of Barbary, are, and always have been, in a habit of trading with them, and felling them Slaves, for the purposes of felling them to the Mahomedans, to serve in their seraglios, and other vile purposes.

IV. That

APPENDIX.

IV. That the greater part of the people refident in the interior parts of Africa breed Slaves for fale, which fact is moft indifputably proved.

V. That before the intercourfe of the people on the Weftern Coaft with the Europeans, they ufed to facrifice and eat one another.

VI. That fuch favage cuftoms are leffened in a confiderable degree fince fuch intercourfe, and there is reafon to believe will continue to diminifh gradually, if fuch intercourfe is continued.

VII. That if the Traffick is abolifhed, there is the ftrongeft reafon to believe the enormities above-mentioned will be renewed, and confequently that the Promoters of the Abolition of the Slave-Trade will be the immediate inftruments of the maffacres, murders, and facrifices which the African Trade at prefent has, in fome meafure, prevented, and would undoubtedly put a ftop to, if continued.

None

APPENDIX.

None of the perfons examined either by the Committee of the Privy Council, or of the Houfe of Commons, have given their teftimony upon oath :—Perfons of the loweft clafs, common failors, who have run from their fhips, difcarded furgeons of African fhips, and other perfons unworthy of belief, feem to have had the fame degree of credit given to them and their tales as have been annexed to the candid accounts of Gentlemen who have long refided on the Coaft in public capacities, to Merchants of reputation, and Captains of fhips, who are ready to atteft on oath every thing they have afferted.

One Gentleman, of the latter defcription, who was not in England laft year when the witneffes were examined before the Committee of the Houfe of Commons, has thought proper to give the following account upon oath.

WILLIAM

APPENDIX.

WILLIAM CRAIG HARBORNE, of Liverpool, in the county of Lancashire, being sworn on the Holy Evangelists of Almighty God, maketh oath, and saith, That he this Deponent hath been concerned and engaged in the Trade to Africa, principally from the Port of Liverpool, for upwards of twenty years last past; and having seen accounts of the manner of carrying on such Trade, and of the manners and customs of the natives of that country, (which appear to him very different from the truth,) which have been circulated through this kingdom, to induce people to join in soliciting the Legislature to abolish such Trade, as inconsistent with the principles of justice and humanity; he has been induced, from a regard to the cause of truth and justice, to his own reputation and that of other mariners and merchants concerned in such Trade, to declare in the most solemn manner, from his knowledge and intercourse with the inhabitants of the Coast, that much the greater number, both of those on the coast and the interior parts of the country, are Slaves; and that a

I   very

very defpotic authority and cruel treatment
are exercifed over the generality of thofe who
are confidered as above that rank by their
fuperiors; and this deponent, in order to give
to the public a juft idea of the condition of the
inhabitants of Africa, faith, about the year
1780, being on board the fhip Molly, John
Kendall, mafter, bound from Liverpool to
Annamaboe, in Africa, in quality of furgeon;
the faid fhip in her voyage down ftopped at a
part of the Coaft called Apollonia, in order to
purchafe gold; and fome time after the faid
fhip was brought to an anchor, the Governor
of the Fort (Mr. Lomax) came on board and
told this Deponent, that there had been a great
facrifice among the Negroes, before the arri-
val of the faid fhip: he informed this Deponent in converfation that the former principal
Cabofhier, named he believes Hamacree, was
dead, and that his fucceffor had made what is
called *Cuftom*, that is facrificed to him, or fup-
plied him with, provifions, wives, fervants,
&c. to attend upon him in the other world;
and this Deponent faith, That the defcription
given

given him by Mr. Lomax of this ceremony was to the following effect :—That a great pit was dug, in which were put various provifions, animal and vegetable, and different kinds of liquors; and to the beſt of ſaid Deponent's recollection, an hundred of the handfomeſt of the natives, men, women, and young people of both ſexes, were placed round the pit—That, on a ſignal given, a man went round and knocked them all on the head, ſo that they fell into the pit, which was afterwards filled up with earth—That one of the muſicians, who was to have attended, being prevented by ſickneſs, he was ſent for, and his throat cut, and he was thrown into the pit with the others to play muſic to the deceaſed Cabofhier in the other world.

And this Deponent further ſaith, He is well acquainted with the countries of Calabar and Bonny, where as great a number of Slaves are purchaſed as on any part of the coaſt, and that the inhabitants of thoſe towns are frequently at war with their neighbours, the

Creek

Creek and Andony men : and this Deponent faith, That he well knows they frequently facrifice the prifoners they take in thefe wars, becaufe, when walking through the town of Bonny, he has been obliged to hold his nofe and ftop his breath, to avoid the horrid ftench of the mangled putrefying limbs hung up in the facred or confecrated hut, called by them the Jao-Jao Houfe.

And this deponent further faith, That being at Calabar, in or about the year 1786, a time when the Creek and Calabar people were at war, he went on board a Liverpool fhip belonging to Meffrs. Hodgfons, commanded by Captain Sutton, a gentleman of very good character, who informed the Deponent (what he had before heard was their cuftom) that thofe people facrifice, cut up, cook and eat their prifoners, and drink the broth made of them in public boilers, and this Deponent has been told and believes they fometimes even drink the blood of their enemies ; and Captain Sutton alfo told this
Deponent,

Deponent, that he would on fhore meet the women and children with this broth in their gourds or calabafhes, and this Deponent going on fhore with the faid Captain Sutton, faw the boiler, and a number of the bones faid to be the remains of thofe prifoners; Captain Sutton further informed this Deponent, that, on remonftrating with the Cabo-fhier, named Hammacree, on fuch iphuman doings, he only replied that *be* did not eat man *himfelf, only the other man* did; and this Deponent further faith, that in about fifteen years acquaintance with the Bonny and Cala-bar Trade, he never remembers an inftance, in which the inhabitants fold any of fuch prifoners, although he has been informed, that a part of fuch prifoners are fometimes fold, and their lives thereby faved. And this Deponent further faith, that he faw the late Warry, King of Bonny, come on board the fhip where he was, that he no fooner en-tered the fhip, than the canoe dropped aftern with a poor fellow; that after running a knife in his belly, they toffed him out of the canoe among

among the fharks, who devoured him. That another time he, this Deponent, faw a trial by the water ordeal : an inhabitant of Bonny named Jamaica, who this Deponent believes was Chief Commander of the war canoes of the place, was accufed of poifoning a principal man of the town, named John Tillibo, which faid Deponent underftands and verily believes, is often done fecretly under the Jao, Jao ; the accufers and the accufed were condemned to fwim acrofs a creek which abounded with fharks, in attempting which, one of the accufers was carried away or devoured by the fharks, and the accufed confequently acquitted.

And this Deponent further faith, when he left Annamaboe in the year 1789, the perfon employed by this Deponent as his broker, to examine the gold brought for fale, which is often counterfeit, or of bafe alloy, named yellow Adam, happening to die of a confumption, an old woman, who was his aunt, was fufpected of being the caufe ; on

account

account of which (he was well informed, and verily believes) they cut her up into pieces, so that her flesh looked like meat in a butcher's shambles; and although the price of two flaves was offered for this old woman, as faid Deponent was informed, and believes to be true, they would not fell her.

And this Deponent further faith, That he is convinced by the eagernefs, which the flaves in general appeared to him to fhew, to be purchafed when they are brought on board, they are apprehenfive of a worfe fate if not fold; and this Deponent faith, that he is perfectly convinced that they eat each other, becaufe it is not uncommon for thofe that are fold, to appear to entertain apprehenfions of being eaten by their purchafers, but, when from kind treatment and the attention paid to their health, and accommodation and comfortable living on board, fuch apprehenfions are removed, they are quite at eafe, and cheerful and happy.

And

APPENDIX.

And this Deponent further faith, That whatever room they may have to fleep in, when on board in the middle paffage, he frequently obferved that they croud together as clofe as they can, for the fake of warmth, and has often taken fteps to prevent it.

And this Deponent further faith, That exclufive of the facts above-mentioned, (except what he learned from Governor Lomax,) which depend on his own perfonal knowledge, he has been informed by other perfons, both Whites and Blacks, whom he has known on the coaft, and whom he conceives to have been worthy of credit, and whofe information he verily believes to be true, that the Cabofhiers, Kings, or principal Men in general, often from ebriety, caprice, or amufement, cruelly torture or put to death their Dependants and Slaves, and fometimes in their walks, to fhew their dexterity, cut off the heads of people, or with poignards ftab them down by the collar-bone into the breaft, endeavouring

to

to penetrate the heart, or practise other wanton acts of cruelty on the innocent paffengers.

That he has been particularly informed by Governor Lomax, and believes, that it is cuftomary in the country about the Cape Apollonia, for people to be put to death by their Mafters and Chiefs, in confequence of dreams, or fuppofed crimes, or from caprice. That the faid Governor had often remonftrated with the before-mentioned Cabofhiers on fuch horrid cruelties.

And this Deponent faith, That he was informed by a Mr. Martin, fecond mate of the faid fhip Molly, Captain Kendall, and believes it to be true: that among other acts of cruelty he, the faid Martin, faw a man at one of their feftivals put to death by binding his hands and feet, and throwing him on the fcorching fands, where he was put to death, by mangling him with a jagged knife at intervals, in order to cut off his head, fo that he

lay rolling and writhing in unfpeakable tor-
ments, for a confiderable time, before he ex-
pired, while they were finging and making
merry, drowning his cries with the noife they
made in exultation at his mifery.

And this Deponent faith, That the following circumftances were related to him by Dr.
Richard Grogan, a phyfician, he believes now
living at Limerick in Ireland, which he, this
Deponent, doubts not the faid Dr. Grogan
will be ready to teftify, to wit,

That about the year 1782, clofe under the
walls of the Englifh Fort, at Cape Coaft, or
Anamaboe, *which, from the Commerce of the
Europeans,* is one of the moft *civilized* parts of
the Coaft, a child dying fuddenly, its death
was imputed to forcery or witchcraft, which
was charged on a poor old woman, who, with
her whole family, was condemned to deftruc-
tion :—The lives of thirty of them however
were faved, by being fold to the fhips flaving
there;

there;—three of her sons were sold to the beforementioned Captain John Kendall, of the Molly; on board which ship the said Dr. Grogan then acted as surgeon: one of them, who spoke English, interceded with Captain Kendall to try to save his mother's life, by purchasing her, who humanely made use of his endeavours, by sending on shore an Officer, with orders to give any price that should be asked for her, although she would not be worth the expence of the freight in the West Indies; but the first object he saw on landing was the bloody head of the woman placed in a wooden dish, and borne on the head of her own sister, whom they obliged to proceed with it to the public market-place.

He was informed, that supposing the Masters of the ships would not give any thing for her, though they were advised by the Governor of the Fort to carry her to them, they cut off her head at the very gate of the Fort, and caused it to be carried through the town.

And

APPENDIX.

And this Deponent faith, That, from the above circumstances, and many others, he verily believes that wars, which are frequent in Africa, are not made for the purpose of procuring Slaves, though in instances it has been said to happen; and he is convinced, that if the Trade should be suddenly abolished by the Europeans, many thousand of people would be sacrificed or put to death, who are now saved and placed in very comfortable situations, and they and their offspring are made happy, and many of them brought to the knowledge of God and the doctrines of Christianity; and that the unqualified abolition of the Trade, would, in his opinion, be injuring the cause of humanity, and tend very much to prevent the future civilization of Africa.

(Signed)

WILLIAM CRAIG HARBORNE.

Sworn before me, at the
Mansion-House, London,
21ft April, 1792,
(Signed)
J. HOPKINS, Mayor.

APPENDIX.

The KING OF DENMARK's ORDINANCE relative to the SLAVE-TRADE, dated at the
Palace of Chriftianfborg, March 16, 1792.

WE, Chriftian the VIIth, by the Grace of God
King of Denmark and Norway, &c. &c. make
known by thefe prefents, that, confidering the circumftances which occur in the Slave-Trade, on the
Coaft of Guinea, and in the Tranfportation of the
Negroes from thence to our Weft-India Iflands, and
impreffed with the idea that it would, in every refpect, be beneficial and profitable, if the Importation
of new Negroes, from the Coaft of Guinea, could
be avoided, and our Weft-India Iflands, in procefs
of time, cultivated by Negroes, born and bred in
the Iflands, accuftomed from their youth, to the
manner of labour, the climate, and the difpofition of
their Mafters : We, in confequence, have made
ferious Enquiries how far and when it might be poffible to accomplifh the Abolition of the faid Trade :
From the refult of thefe Enquiries, we are convinced that it is poffible, and will be advantageous
to our Weft-India Iflands, to defift from the farther
Purchafe of new Negroes, *when once the Plantations*
are ftocked with a fufficient Number for Propagation,
and the Cultivation of the Lands ; when pecuniary
affiftance can be given to thofe who want to purchafe Negroes for their Eftates, and if proper encouragement were to be given to Marriage amongft
the Negroes, and due attention paid to their In-
ftruction and Morals.

In.

APPENDIX.

In order, therefore, to withdraw our Weft-India Poffeffions from the State of Dependence, under which they have hitherto been and now are, with refpect to the Importation of Negroes, and to make the Importation of Negroes unneceffary in future, We declare our moft gracious Will on this Subject, and order as follows:

I. From the commencement of the year 1803, We forbid any of our fubjects to carry on the Slave-Trade, from the Coaft of Africa, or any other Place, except in our Weft-India Iflands; fo that, after that period, no Negro Men or Women, either from that Coaft, or other foreign Places, will be allowed to be purchafed by or for our Subjects, or to be tranfported in our Subjects Ships, neither muft they be brought to our Weft-India Iflands for Sale; and every tranfaction, contrary to this prohibition, fhall, after that period, be deemed unlawful.

II. In the mean time, from the prefent until the end of the year 1802, it is permitted to all foreign Nations, without exception and under all flags, to import Negro Men and Women from the Coaft to our Weft-India Iflands.

III. For every healthy and ftout Negro Man or Woman, which, during that period, is thus imported to our Weft-India Iflands, we permit the following quantities of raw fugar to be exported from our Iflands to foreign Places, either in our own or foreign Ships, within a year after the importation of fuch Negroes; viz. for every full-grown Negro Man or Woman, 2,000lb. weight may be exported, and

for

APPENDIX.

for every half-grown Negro, the half of that quantity, or 1,000lb. weight, without any Difference with regard to Sex; but nothing is allowed for the Importation of Children.

IV. The Duty which is fixed by the Ordinances of the 9th of April, 1764, and 12th of May, 1777, (which Ordinances in every other respect, that regards the Slave-Trade, are hereby repealed,) on the Importation of Slaves, We most graciously take off, with regard to the Negroe-Women which may be hereafter imported; but, on the other hand, We impose a Duty of ¼ per Cent. more than what is already stipulated on the Sugars, which shall be exported to foreign Places, for the Purchase of such Negroe Men or Women as are imported.

V. It is moreover our Will, in order to establish an exact Proportion among the different Sexes, that, from the beginning of 1795 and after, the Negroe Women and Girls, who work in the Field and are not House Negroes, shall pay no Poll-Tax; but, on the contrary, from the above-mentioned period, a double Poll-Tax shall be exacted for every Negroe Man.

VI. From the present period, We forbid, in the strongest manner, all Exportation of Negroe Men or Women from our West-India Islands, they alone being excepted from this Prohibition, who are expelled by Law; or, such as our Governor-General and Council in the West Indies may upon very extraordinary occasions think proper, according to circumstances, to permit to depart.

Wherefore

APPENDIX.

Wherefore this our Royal Will being made known, We order all and every one to conform to it.

Given at our Palace of Chriftianfborg, in our Royal Place of Refidence, Copenhagen, the 16th of March, 1792.

Under our Royal Hand and Seal.

C. R.

———————————————

SCHEEL.   HAGERUP.   TRANT.

ROSENSTAND.   GOISCKE.

to penetrate the heart, or practise other wanton acts of cruelty on the innocent passengers.

That he has been particularly informed by Governor Lomax, and believes, that it is customary in the country about the Cape Apollonia, for people to be put to death by their Masters and Chiefs, in consequence of dreams, or supposed crimes, or from caprice. That the said Governor had often remonstrated with the before-mentioned Cabothiers on such horrid cruelties.

And this Deponent saith, That he was informed by a Mr. Martin, second mate of the said ship Molly, Captain Kendall, and believes it to be true: that among other acts of cruelty he, the said Martin, saw a man at one of their festivals put to death by binding his hands and feet, and throwing him on the scorching sands, where he was put to death, by mangling him with a jagged knife at intervals, in order to cut off his head, so that he

K   lay

lay rolling and writhing in unfpeakable tor-
ments, for a confiderable time, before he ex-
pired, while they were finging and making
merry, drowning his cries with the noife they
made in exultation at his mifery.

And this Deponent faith, That the following circumftances were related to him by Dr.
Richard Grogan, a phyfician, he believes now
living at Limerick in Ireland, which he, this
Deponent, doubts not the faid Dr. Grogan
will be ready to teftify, to wit,

That about the year 1782, clofe under the
walls of the Englifh Fort, at Cape Coaft, or
Anamaboe, *which, from the Commerce of the
Europeans,* is one of the moft *civilized* parts of
the Coaft, a child dying fuddenly, its death
was imputed to forcery or witchcraft, which
was charged on a poor old woman, who, with
her whole family, was condemned to deftruc-
tion:—The lives of thirty of them however
were faved, by being fold to the fhips flaving
there;

there;—three of her fons were fold to the beforementioned Captain John Kendall, of the
Molly; on board which ſhip the ſaid Dr.
Grogan then acted as ſurgeon: one of them,
who ſpoke Engliſh, interceded with Captain
Kendall to try to ſave his mother's life, by
purchaſing her, who humanely made uſe of
his endeavours, by ſending on ſhore an Officer,
with orders to give any price that ſhould be
aſked for her, although ſhe would not be
worth the expence of the freight in the Weſt
Indies; but the firſt object he ſaw on landing
was the bloody head of the woman placed in a
wooden diſh, and borne on the head of her
own ſiſter, whom they obliged to proceed with
it to the public market-place.

He was informed, that ſuppoſing the Maſ-
ters of the ſhips would not give any thing for
her, though they were adviſed by the Governor of the Fort to carry her to them, they cut
off her head at the very gate of the Fort, and
cauſed it to be carried through the town.

APPENDIX.

And this Deponent faith, That, from the above circumſtances, and many others, he verily believes that wars, which are frequent in Africa, are not made for the purpoſe of procuring Slaves, though in inſtances it has been ſaid to happen; and he is convinced, that if the Trade ſhould be ſuddenly aboliſhed by the Europeans, many thouſand of people would be ſacrificed or put to death, who are now ſaved and placed in very comfortable ſituations, and they and their offspring are made happy, and many of them brought to the knowledge of God and the doctrines of Chriſtianity; and that the unqualified abolition of the Trade, would, in his opinion, be injuring the cauſe of humanity, and tend very much to prevent the future civilization of Africa.

(Signed)

WILLIAM CRAIG HARBORNE.

Sworn before me, at the
Manſion-Houſe, London,
21ſt April, 1792,
(Signed)
J. HOPKINS, Mayor.

APPENDIX.

The KING OF DENMARK's ORDINANCE relative to the SLAVE-TRADE, dated at the
Palace of Christiansborg, March 16, 1792.

WE, Christian the VIIth, by the Grace of God
King of Denmark and Norway, &c. &c. make
known by these presents, that, considering the circumstances which occur in the Slave-Trade, on the
Coast of Guinea, and in the Transportation of the
Negroes from thence to our West-India Islands, and
impressed with the idea that it would, in every respect, be beneficial and profitable, if the Importation
of new Negroes, from the Coast of Guinea, could
be avoided, and our West-India Islands, in process
of time, cultivated by Negroes, born and bred in
the Islands, accustomed from their youth, to the
manner of labour, the climate, and the disposition of
their Masters : We, in consequence, have made
serious Enquiries how far and when it might be possible to accomplish the Abolition of the said Trade :
From the result of these Enquiries, we are convinced that it is possible, and will be advantageous
to our West-India Islands, to desist from the farther
Purchase of new Negroes, *when once the Plantations*
are stocked with a sufficient Number for Propagation,
and the Cultivation of the Lands ; when pecuniary
assistance can be given to those who want to purchase Negroes for their Estates, and if proper encouragement were to be given to Marriage amongst
the Negroes, and due attention paid to their In-
struction and Morals.

In

APPENDIX.

In order, therefore, to withdraw our Weft-India Poffeffions from the State of Dependence, under which they have hitherto been and now are, with refpect to the Importation of Negroes, and to make the Importation of Negroes unneceffary in future, We declare our moft gracious Will on this Subject, and order as follows :

I. From the commencement of the year 1803, We forbid any of our fubjects to carry on the Slave-Trade, from the Coaft of Africa, or any other Place, except in our Weft-India Iflands ; fo that, after that period, no Negro Men or Women, eithei from that Coaft, or other foreign Places, will be allowed to be purchafed by or for our Subjects, or to be tranf-ported in our Subjects Ships, neither muft they be brought to our Weft-India Iflands for Sale; and every tranfaction, contrary to this prohibition, fhall, after that period, be deemed unlawful.

II. In the mean time, from the prefent until the end of the year 1802, it is permitted to all foreign Nations, without exception and under all flags, to import Negro Men and Women from the Coaft to our Weft-India Iflands.

III. For every healthy and ftout Negro Man or Woman, which, during that period, is thus imported to our Weft-India Iflands, we permit the following quantities of raw fugar to be exported from our Iflands to foreign Places, either in our own or fo-reign Ships, within a year after the importation of fuch Negroes ; viz. for every full-grown Negro Man or Woman, 2,000lb. weight may be exported, and

fo

APPENDIX.

for every half-grown Negro, the half of that quantity, or 1,000lb. weight, without any Difference with regard to Sex; but nothing is allowed for the Importation of Children.

IV. The Duty which is fixed by the Ordinances of the 9th of April, 1764, and 12th of May, 1777, (which Ordinances in every other respect, that regards the Slave-Trade, are hereby repealed,) on the Importation of Slaves, We most graciously take off, with regard to the Negroe-Women which may be hereafter imported; but, on the other hand, We impose a Duty of ¼ per Cent. more than what is already stipulated on the Sugars, which shall be exported to foreign Places, for the Purchase of such Negroe Men or Women as are imported.

V. It is moreover our Will, in order to establish an exact Proportion among the different Sexes, that, from the beginning of 1795 and after, the Negroe Women and Girls, who work in the Field and are not House Negroes, shall pay no Poll-Tax; but, on the contrary, from the above-mentioned period, a double Poll-Tax shall be exacted for every Negroe Man.

VI. From the present period, We forbid, in the strongest manner, all Exportation of Negroe Men or Women from our West-India Islands, they alone being excepted from this Prohibition, who are expelled by Law; or, such as our Governor-General and Council in the West Indies may upon very extraordinary occasions think proper, according to circumstances, to permit to depart.

Wherefore

APPENDIX.

Wherefore this our Royal Will being made known, We order all and every one to conform to it.

Given at our Palace of Chriftianfborg, in our Royal Place of Refidence, Copenhagen, the 16th of March, 1792.

Under our Royal Hand and Seal.

C. R.

SCHEEL.   HAGERUP.   TRANT.

ROSENSTAND.   GOISCKE.